The Vow She Couldn't Keep

Girls' Romance stories

TENDER HEARTS

The Vow She Couldn't Keep

by Marguerite Whitehead

TABLE OF CONTENTS

Chapter One

NO DATES . . . NO BOYS

At the beginning of her second week at college Julie Winters walked into the building with far more confidence than she'd had the previous week when she'd been a 'new girl'. She was familiar with the routine now, the moving from one part of the building to another for each session, the various tutors and the subjects so different from those she'd been taking at school.

She walked down the long corridor linking the Technical Section with the Commerce Department, glancing briefly in the Domestic Science Room at the girls and boys, rolling pastry or stirring the contents of pans. They were the cooks and chefs of the future. There was always a lovely aroma coming from here tempting her to pause for a few seconds before continuing on down the corridor. Further down she came to the

Electrical Engineering Room but she knew better now than to look in as she had on her first day. She'd stopped then to look at the boys working in there, some wearing shields to protect their eyes from the sparks flying from the tools they were using.

Suddenly, all eyes were on her as she stood framed in the doorway. Machines were switched off and the silence was broken by a simultaneous wolf whistle. The boy nearest to her had raised his protective goggles to stare at her admiringly with twinkling brown eyes.

"Wow," he said before Julie, high heels clickety-clicking, fled round the corner to the Commerce Department. That unknown boy had disconcerted her. His cheeky smile didn't fit the image she was creating for herself. Julie intended leaving college in a year's time as a fully trained secretary but that was only the first stepping-stone. One day she'd be Personal Assistant to an important person, perhaps a fashion designer or a television producer. Those were her dreams and she was determined to make them come true.

Julie took her place at her desk noticing that the one next to her was still empty as it had been all her first week. She smiled at her friend Cathy, sitting on her left, lifted the lid of her desk, opened her instruction book and the lesson began.

After a few moments, Miss Compton, the tutor, said with a frown, "You're all typing erratically."

Julie kept her eyes on her book and was unaware that someone had slipped into the empty desk beside her until a voice murmured, "Wouldn't be so bad if she'd smile now and again, would it?"

The voice was a boy's. Startled, Julie glanced sideways to see a very good-looking young man sitting there. In spite of being the only boy in the room he appeared to be completely unembarrassed as he looked at her admiringly.

At eleven o'clock there was a break before the students went into the shorthand class. Julie and Cathy walked with the others to the refectory and took their places in the queue for the coffee vending machine.

"Who's the dishy bloke next to you?" Cathy asked.

"I haven't a clue."

"Well don't let him distract you," Cathy warned.

"There's not a chance – this is a strictly no boy year."

"Oh yes, I believe you," laughed Cathy. Julie was slightly annoyed that her friend was not taking her seriously. "I mean it, Cathy. I've got to concentrate on my work. This is going to be a no boy, no date year!"

All the tables were full and Cathy and Julie took their plastic cups to the window and sat on the sill.

"I wouldn't mind getting to know him," Cathy said, reverting to the subject of their previous conversation. "But just you see, there'll be no chance of any of us doing that when Madeleine sets eyes on him."

Madeleine, one of the prettiest and most outgoing among the students, collected boys as some girls add charms to their bracelets. The two girls watched as the young man took his coffee then stood looking round as if wondering which group to approach.

"Try to look friendly at least," Cathy said, "after all it's his first day and he's bound to feel a bit out of things when the rest of us have already settled in."

The boy didn't appear to need encouragement however. Slowly his eyes travelled round the room and finally came to rest on Julie. Immediately he began to walk towards the two girls and Julie noticed how attractive he was with longish blond hair, well cut, and combed over his forehead. He was neatly dressed in a grey suit the same colour as his eyes. The fingers which held his coffee cup looked as if they'd never lifted anything heavier than a knife and fork.

"My name's Craig Merton," he said. "What's yours?"

"Julie Winters."

"Julie, – Mm, suits you."

"And this is Cathy."

The boy glanced briefly and without interest at Cathy then back to Julie, the admiration in his eyes making her wonder if her 'no boy year' resolution was such a good idea after all.

The bell rang indicating the end of the break and the girls were walking back down the corridor again when they were nearly swept off their feet by a huddle of boys coming from the Engineering Room. One caught hold of Julie and steadied her and she looked up into teasing brown eyes which looked vaguely familiar.

"You're not bad," he said, "not at all bad."

She recognised him now. He was the boy who'd embarrassed her with his wolf whistle on her first day. She pushed his hands from her arms, but knew that he watched her as she walked away.

In spite of her resolution not to let anything interfere with her studies, Julie was constantly aware of Craig's presence in the typing room. Some instinct told her he was watching her as her fingers became more flexible and flew over the typewriter keys. Several other girls in the class seemed eager to get to know him and he was usually surrounded by admiring teenagers during each break time. Julie was glad that she didn't see him in any of her other classes – he was far too distracting.

"Why don't you give him a bit of encouragement?" Cathy asked one day.

"I've told you, I've no time to spare for boys at the moment. I'm determined to concentrate on this course.

"Well, I'll bet you don't succeed, not with your looks – he's obviously attracted to you." She smiled without envy. "I wish I had the chance."

A few days later Miss Compton told them about the Students' Union.

"There's a meeting tonight and two representatives

14

will be chosen from each class. I'd like you all to go because various other committees will be formed and there'll be something there for everyone of you I'm sure. Go along and put your ideas forward."

She was young and her enthusiasm was contagious. Most of the students were at the meeting that evening.

Craig and Madeleine were chosen to represent the typing classes.

"It's obvious they would be," Cathy said, "they're both oozing with confidence."

Julie noticed that the boy with the brown eyes was elected from the engineering students and was surprised at the cheers which greeted the announcement. He was obviously popular among his fellow students.

The girls parted at the end of the college drive to go their separate ways but soon Julie heard hurrying footsteps behind her. It was Craig.

"I'll walk home with you, Julie," he said, "I'm going your way."

"How do you know where I live?"

"I took a peep in the register," he replied.

Here was a chance to satisfy her curiosity.

"Why are you learning typing, Craig?"

"I'm going to be a reporter," he replied. "I'm taking shorthand too, but not in the same class as you – I'm a bit more advanced, I've been going to evening school for some time."

"A reporter! Sounds exciting. Will you have to investigate crimes?"

"I don't intend being a reporter for very long," Craig replied, "this is just the beginning."

"You're like me – ambitious."

"Yes, I think we're two of a kind you and me, Julie."

"You might not think that when you know me better."

"That sounds like a promise." When she didn't reply, he went on, "Do you want to know me better?"

"Maybe, some day."

Julie's young sister, Emma, was watching for her through the window and when Julie entered the house, she asked, "Who was that? He looked like a film star."

"Only a boy from the college walking home the same way as me, so don't go jumping to conclusions." As soon as Emma saw her with a boy she began to think of engagement rings.

There was another meeting at the college a few days later, this time for all those interested in forming a social committee with a view to arranging events for charities. Both Julie and Cathy were elected to the committee and to Julie's dismay the annoying boy with the brown eyes was Chairman.

"I think I'll resign," Julie said to Cathy.

"You're not leaving me without some support, Julie. If you go, so do I."

"All right, I'll stay but keep him out of my hair."

They discovered that he was called Matthew Dunning, popularly known as Matt, that he was seventeen and a half and was studying electronics and computers. Julie immediately sensed some antagonism between him and Craig by the way they looked and spoke to each other.

Several things were decided at the meeting. The college was to have a summer event with the proceeds going to charity. Smaller committees were formed and several ideas put forward.

A boy called Andrew suggested a sponsored walk round the football field but Matt thought it too ordinary.

"It's old hat," he said. "Come on girls, can't one of *you* come up with something more original?" He was looking directly at Julie. "What about a dancing marathon? Something more personal," someone suggested.

Matt was still looking at Julie and she felt obliged to answer.

"I prefer the walk," she said, "because it *is* impersonal."

"I see. Would you prefer us to have two walks, one for the boys and the other for the girls? Would that be impersonal enough for you?" Matt asked.

He was teasing she knew, but he infuriated her.

No one offered an alternative, so the walk was decided on and most of the students put their names down for the event.

"What about you, Craig?" Matt asked.

"Not my scene," Craig replied. "Surely you can find better ways of raising money than by walking round and round a football field?"

"You'd rather be playing football, I suppose," Matt said.

"You know very well I don't play."

Julie could feel the atmosphere between them and was glad when Andrew quickly put forward another suggestion.

"Let's make it a proper walk," he said, "with definite starting and ending places instead of round a field. We can be sponsored for so much a mile and for those who reach the target there can be a reward, perhaps a meal or a disco at the end of it."

"I don't think many of us will feel like discoing if

we've walked ten miles or so," Matt said, "but it's a great idea. We'll start from college and fix the end of the walk later. And we'll have a slap-up meal at the end for those who stay the course. That should give us an incentive."

"And how do we get back?" Cathy asked.

Craig said quickly, "Knowing Matt, he probably expects you to slog back on shank's pony, the same way you get there."

"Transport will be arranged for the return journey," Matt said, "and knowing you I don't think you'll want to miss the meal, Craig, so if you won't walk there you can get on your bike." The words sounded like an insult. The two boys glared at each other for a moment but in the end the idea was agreed on and Andrew was put in charge of the arrangements.

There was to be a full week of events and many other money-making ideas were put forward, some were rejected, others accepted. Someone suggested forming a college magazine and Madeleine proposed Craig as the editor. There was no opposition and Craig was obviously delighted. Julie gave him a 'thumbs up' sign and noticed that Matt was watching her with a quizzical expression.

"We want some good ideas for the open days," Matt

said. "The college will be thrown open to our vast public of doting parents and admiring relatives so we want escorts to show them round. Offers from anyone able to make polite small talk will be welcome."

Colleen, the college's chatterbox, put up her hand and everyone laughed. Cathy suggested she and Julie ought to offer as it might release them from more unpleasant tasks. Rather reluctantly Julie put her hand up and Matt asked for their names and telephone numbers.

"Julie Winters," she said.

"Ah, that accounts for it."

"Accounts for what?"

"Your coldness," he said. "You're living up to your name."

"Not a very original remark," Julie said.

Nothing seemed to perturb him, he was still smiling as he said, "Maybe not, but apt, wouldn't you say?"

Julie turned to Cathy and whispered, "Why on earth did they choose someone like him to be Social Sec?"

"He's got what it takes," Cathy whispered back.

"Such as?"

"Well, drive, enthusiasm – he gets people going."

"He certainly gets me going."

The two girls became aware that there was complete silence in the room and looking at the platform Julie saw

Matt with half a smile on his lips waiting for them to stop talking.

"If you've finished your little discussion we'll continue with the meeting."

How dare he draw attention to her like that, Julie fumed, wishing she could stalk out of the room then asking herself why should she miss out on anything just because of one cocky, clever individual. Far better to beat him at his own game.

Miss Compton and several teachers joined the meeting then and other ideas were approved. There would be a Fair with the usual side shows, and exhibitions in the college itself. Demonstrations of keep-fit, and judo would take place and a cafe with special dishes made by the domestic science students, would be open. But the idea which caused the most excitement was a suggestion from Miss Compton, that a Drama Society be formed. As she was also Head of English Department, she would be in charge of that and wanted to get enrolments immediately. Madeleine's was the first name down.

"I did a bit of acting at school," she said, "and my mum was on the stage once." She ran a hand through her auburn hair, her pretty face alight with enthusiasm.

"I can already see the headlines," Matt said, pretending to read an imaginary paper, "college student becomes star overnight."

Madeleine turned a furious face towards him, "Your sarcasm is wasted on me, Matthew Dunning, so belt up."

His face was the picture of innocence as he said, "I mean it, Maddy, you're star material. Isn't she, Miss Compton?"

Madeleine's name was put on Miss Compton's list along with Craig's, Andrew's and about a dozen others.

"You can't all be given parts," the tutor said, "some of you will have more mundane jobs such as stage managers or scene shifters, and we'll want some artists from the art class to paint the scenery, also those with the know-how to see to the lighting."

"You can put me down for that," Matt said, then casting a wicked glance at Madeleine he murmured, "I'll see that the spotlight falls right on you, Maddy."

Three girls and two boys from the fashion design department offered to make costumes for the play, "as long as it's not a period drama, I don't fancy making crinolines," Douglas, one of the boys, said.

"No, we'll keep it simple," Miss Compton promised. She looked at Cathy and Julie, "What about you two. Don't you fancy doing a bit of acting?"

"I can't spare the time, Miss Compton," Julie

explained, "with all the homework and the reading up each night . . ."

"Oh come, dear. All work you know . . . you must have some relaxation too."

"You can be my assistant," Matt said.

Julie ignored him. "I'll be the prompter or something backstage then," she offered, "but I don't want to have to learn any lines."

The meeting ended with everyone leaving, already making plans for the events they'd offered to help with. Cathy, Julie and Andrew were walking along the drive and Julie could see Madeleine and Craig ahead of them talking animatedly. She felt a little twinge of regret that she wasn't the one walking with Craig, but pushed it down resolutely.

A footstep crunched on the gravel behind her and a hand was slipped through her arm. It was Matthew. Quickly she shook her arm free, wishing that Cathy had not continued walking on with Andrew.

"Why didn't our little hedgehog want to go on stage?"

"*You* call *me* a hedgehog!"

"Well, you are a bit prickly aren't you?"

"You're so, so . . ."

"Go on say it. Cocky. That's what my mum calls me when she's ticking me off."

"I imagine she has to do that pretty often."

Matt merely laughed. She realised that he rarely seemed to get annoyed – except with Craig – and she wondered why.

By now they'd reached the main road. Andrew said 'goodbye' and went in the other direction but Matt continued to walk along with Julie and Cathy and talk became general. Matt told them about his plans. He already had a job lined up and would soon be working for two days a week and spending the rest of the time in college. He talked enthusiastically about computers, electronics, and other things the girls had never been interested in but his eagerness came over clearly.

"It sounds complicated," Cathy said, "wouldn't you rather go for an office job?"

Matthew roared with laughter. "Me! A pen-pusher. Not likely."

"It sounds practical and looks hard work," Julie said.

"So you actually notice me when you walk past our classroom door?"

The teasing note was back in his voice again but Julie ignored it. They'd reached the end of the road where she lived now and Matt walked on with Cathy.

Poor Cathy, she thought, having to put up with him for another five minutes.

Chapter Two

SO UNROMANTIC

A few days later, Julie was sitting in her room transcribing her shorthand notes into longhand when Emma called upstairs, "Phone, for you, Julie."

Julie ran downstairs thinking it would be Cathy perhaps wanting help with her own shorthand, but was surprised when a masculine voice said, "That you, Julie?"

"Craig." Her heart fluttered.

"Can you see me tonight? There's something I want to talk to you about."

Disappointment welled inside her. This didn't sound like a date, more like someone else wanting help with homework.

"You'll see me at college on Friday," she said.

"It's now I want to talk to you. We don't get together

much in college, do we?"

In spite of her resolution not to be side-tracked, Julie found herself weakening. She couldn't miss the opportunity of having Craig to herself for a couple of hours – there wasn't a girl in her class who would throw away a chance like that.

"Meet me at Brello's Coffee Bar in an hour," Craig said.

That gave her time to put on the new make-up she'd bought. She wore a dark-blue all-in-one suit, and wrapped a white, woolly scarf round her neck for the night was chilly. Craig was already in the coffee bar when she arrived.

She stood for a moment looking at him through the window. The light above the table made his hair shine like gold. He wore a white and blue sweater with a medallion round his neck. He was certainly the best looking boy she'd ever met and her heart flipped over.

"Don't kid yourself, Julie," she said to herself sternly, "he's only asked you to meet him to talk about the magazine he's editing." But another thought crept into her mind. Could her plans not to date this year hold fast if he asked her to go out with him?

Slipping into the seat opposite him she said, "You can't be wanting help with your shorthand, Craig, seeing that you're already taking down at about 1,000 words a minute. So what did you want to see me about?"

To her surprise, he took her remark seriously.

"You're quite right, Julie – shorthand comes easy to me."

"What is it then?"

He brought her coffee and a doughnut before he replied. "You know I've been made editor of the college magazine we're going to bring out . . . well . . . I wondered if you'd help me with the typing?"

Julie's heart sank, "But you're good at typing, Craig."

"I know, but I couldn't possibly do it all, I've got my own work to do, remember. And I don't want to be reading other people's work all the time . . . I'll write the editorial . . . that'll be good practice for me."

"Is that why you took on the job of editor?"

"Partly . . ." He looked at her, his grey eyes pleading, melting her resolve. He really was too attractive for his own good – and her's.

"I'll help all I can, Craig, of course I will, but I've got to get on with my own work too."

Craig reached over the table and placed his hand over hers. She noted the long, tapering fingers and the well-groomed nails, and electric tingles seemed to run from his fingers into hers.

"That's my girl," Craig said, "I knew you wouldn't let me down."

Something made her glance at the doorway and she saw Matt standing there staring directly at them. The scene must have looked romantic, boy and girl looking into each other's eyes, Craig's hand holding her's. "Let him think what he likes," Julie thought. "It might keep him out of my way."

She smiled happily at Matt, then began talking animatedly to Craig. When she next glanced at the door Matt had gone.

"I won't be able to do all the typing, Craig," Julie said, "but some of the others could help, couldn't they?"

Craig took his hand away from hers and sipped his coffee before replying. "I must have someone I can depend on, Julie," he said, "like you."

Julie thought how she would have liked him to say she was pretty or even good company, but 'dependable', it sounded so unromantic. 'Don't be an idiot' the small inward voice said. 'Romance is the last thing you want, remember?' In spite of that she felt disappointed.

"Perhaps Cathy will help out," she suggested.

"Yes. I'd already thought of that. Will you ask her, Julie?"

"And what about Madeleine?"

Craig's face brightened. "Maddy wouldn't have the time. She's a dead cert to play leading lady in the play."

"Well I'll have to work hard too, Craig, even if it's only to pass the exams."

"You'll pass easily – you're good. Miss Compton said so." He popped the last bit of doughnut into his mouth and wiped the sugar off his hands with a paper napkin. "Besides, it's not so important for you, is it? Typists' jobs are easy to come by."

Julie screwed her napkin into a tight ball. "It's just as important for me as it is for you. And it's not any old typing job I'm after. I'm . . ."

Craig interrupted. "Please, Julie, don't start on women's lib and all that rot." He picked up her scarf and tied it gently round her neck, touching her cheek lingeringly as he did so. "I chose you because you're the only one I know won't let me down."

Julie felt as if she was being twisted round his little finger and wished she could say so but she couldn't.

Craig saw her on to a bus but didn't take her all the way home.

She waved to him from the bus and settled down to her own thoughts. She felt twisted up inside as if an argument between two people was going on inside her head. Her practical side reminded her of the resolutions she'd made before beginning at the college, to keep her mind on the end product . . . a good job. Her other, sentimental side, told her that she'd be downright silly to miss this opportunity of getting to know Craig better. Every girl in her section would give her back teeth to have the chance which had been handed to her.

In the end she made a compromise. She wouldn't neglect her studies, for Craig who was so ambitious himself wouldn't admire her if she did, but somehow, she'd find time to help him with the magazine. And she consoled herself with the thought that it would all be good experience for both Craig and herself.

Julie's last thought before falling asleep that night was of how wonderful it would be if both she and Craig ended up working for the same newspaper. And perhaps some day he would achieve his ambition of being an editor and she'd be his personal assistant – and hopefully, too, the most important girl in Craig's life.

Chapter Three

JEALOUS GUY

There were meetings of one kind or another on two or three nights each week now and Julie and Cathy wondered how they'd ever filled their pre-college days. Apart from homework they were play-reading to find the most suitable drama for the college to produce. Discussion groups were planning other forms of entertainment for the fair as well as making arrangements for the open days and other smaller events.

The walk was well-sponsored with most of the local firms backing at least one contestant and the families and friends of those taking part also agreeing to pay a fixed amount for each mile covered.

The length was twelve miles, easy going at first but with some rough terrain about mid-way and an uphill climb for the last two miles. Whenever possible the 'walkers' practised, trotting round the large grounds of the college and scorning buses on the way to and from the college.

Andrew, in charge of the event, was a hard taskmaster and made sure as far as he could that each of the students taking part would be fit enough to finish the course.

"It's all right for you," Cathy said to him one day, "your legs are about nine inches longer than ours so you don't have to make as many strides as we do. Therefore you're not walking as far."

Everyone laughed. "Get out of that one, Andrew," Matt said.

Julie had seen Matt only at the meetings recently and had the feeling that even there he'd tried to avoid being alone with her. She'd noticed the change in him ever since the evening he'd seen her with Craig in the coffee bar. Even Cathy noticed it. "What's wrong with Matt?" she asked one day. "He always looks at you the way people look when they're saying 'Goodbye' to someone."

"Jolly good thing, too," Julie said, "it saves me having to keep snubbing him."

"But he's a great organiser, Julie – you must admit that. He's got even the laziest of us doing something.

His enthusiasm rubs off on us."

"Enthusiasm! So that's what you call it. Well it only rubs *me* up the wrong way."

Cathy stared at her friend. "I'll remind you of that some day."

"What's that supposed to mean?"

"Oh nothing . . . forget it."

Andrew called them at that moment. "There's a group of us going jogging round the park tonight." He patted Cathy's slender shoulders and said, "Must get you in trim for the big day. Meet us at the park gates at 5.30 pm. That'll just about give you time to get your jogging suits on."

Julie walked towards the park, wishing Craig had been going too. Madeleine had refused to take part in the walk. For Julie, jogging with Craig beside her would have turned a chore into a pleasure.

The group of boys and girls waiting at the gates gave a cheer as she approached and she saw Matt glance at his watch. "Only three minutes late," he said, "but we'll not argue about that."

"That's big of you," she said, sarcastically.

"Cheer up, Julie," Cathy said, "Craig's coming too."

The next moment Craig was standing beside her.

"Surprise, surprise – I thought you hated walking."

"I don't *hate* it, Julie, I merely think it's easier to ride than walk. Joggers are usually a lot of cranks."

"Then why are you coming?"

"I've decided to go on the walk after all. I thought I'd write up a piece about it afterwards."

"For the magazine?"

"Yes. Something newsworthy might happen, you never know."

"Craig! Don't tell me you're hoping one of us will have an accident," she teased, but as always Craig took her words seriously. "Of course not . . . but you never know do you? Hopefully we might encounter something unusual on the way." He smiled in his charming way, "Keep with me, will you, Julie, at least your company will add a touch of spice."

Julie wondered if he'd have wanted her beside him if Madeleine had been there. Madeleine had been making a dead set for him during the past week and few boys were able to resist her.

Matt came up to them then. "I hope you two have got sensible shoes on," he said staring at Julie's feet. "Well, at least they're better than those high heels you go clicking down the corridors on."

"Get lost, Matt . . . you're not the organiser of this."

"And we don't need your advice," Craig said.

They set off in twos and threes at a steady pace, round the bowling greens, along wooded walks, to the gate on the far side of the park. Some dropped out after a time and Cathy stopped to take a stone out of her shoe. As Julie reached her she said, "It's fatal to sit down, Julie, you'd better keep on and I'll join you on the way back."

Julie would have been glad of the excuse to stop but felt obliged to keep going. However, after a few yards, Craig caught her arm.

"It's hardly fair to leave Cathy alone, is it? Let's stay with her and tag on to them again when they come back."

Matt and Andrew were well in front and seeing their retreating backs Julie stopped running and walked back to Cathy.

"Better not let Matt know you stopped," she said, and Julie saw a flash of temper cross Craig's face. "I don't have to account to him for anything I do. In any case Andrew's the organiser of the walk not *him*."

He said the last word with such contempt that Julie looked at him in surprise. "Have you known each other long, Craig?" she asked.

"Too long," he replied curtly. "Steer clear of him, Julie, he's a trouble maker, as I know to my cost."

She longed to know more but didn't like to ask. Cathy

said, "Trouble over a girl, was it?"

"I'd rather not discuss it," Craig replied. "Let's find a pleasanter subject than Matt Dunning to talk about, shall we?"

After ten minutes the joggers returned, Matt and Andrew well in front of the rest. As they drew level Matt said, "Enjoy your little rest?"

"We stopped to keep Cathy company," Julie said as they fell in behind Andrew and Matt.

"Really?" The surprise in Matt's voice was obviously put on for effect. "You've not always been ready to help a lady in distress, have you, Craig?"

"Clear off, will you!" Craig shouted angrily, and Julie realised that the antagonism between the two boys had a far deeper origin than a mere clash of temperaments.

They dispersed at the park gates. Craig got on a bus, Matt, Andrew, Cathy and Julie walked along together, until Cathy came to the road where she lived and Andrew said he'd walk with her to her door.

Matt and Julie strolled along awkwardly. It was the first time they'd been entirely alone for several weeks and Julie was inwardly seething at what she felt was Matt's rudeness to Craig. After walking in silence for a few moments Matt said, "You did well, Julie . . . a lot of the girls dropped out."

"Gosh. That's praise, coming from you."

"I give it where it's due."

They walked without speaking again until they reached the road which Matt should have taken but he continued to walk along with her.

"You needn't come any further," Julie said.

Matt's smile was a bit crooked. "And here am I thinking you'd be glad of my company." Julie didn't reply and, obviously trying to ease the tension, he went on, "My mum says I must always be a perfect gentleman and see my girl friends right to their front doors."

"I'm hardly that, am I? Your girl friend, I mean."

"Well . . . not yet . . . but there's time, we're both young," Matt said airily.

"What else does your mum teach you? Obviously, not to forgive your enemies." There was a tinge of bitterness in Julie's voice and Matt pulled her round to face him.

"Look, Julie, I'll admit I don't care for Craig much, but that's no reason for you and me not to be friends."

She stared up at him. It was dusk now and the street lights had come on, bringing out glints of red in his brown hair. He looked strong and capable and something else – dependable. The right kind of person to have as a friend. Yet how could she make a friend of

someone who disliked Craig? Aloud she said, "Why don't you like Craig? Could it be that you're jealous of him, Matt?"

He looked at her for a moment before answering then said quietly, "Hardly that, Julie, under the circumstances."

They stared at each other for a moment then the familiar twinkle appeared in Matt's eyes as he said, "But it's just possible I could get jealous if you give him too much of your time."

"Are you never serious?"

"Right now, I'm dead serious," Matt said.

Chapter Four

—⟶⟶≈✦≈⟵⟵—

KISS AND STRUGGLE

"Gosh, I'm hungry, Mum," Julie said as she entered the house and caught the whiff of potato pie coming from the oven.

"No wonder, after running round the park several times," Mrs Winters said.

"Who was the boy who brought you home?" asked Emma, and her mother looked up.

"Only a boy from the college." Julie pulled one of Emma's plaits. "So don't start making up stories about him."

Emma wanted to be a novelist and romanticised everything. "Is he nice?" she asked.

"Well – could be if he tried, I suppose."

"And doesn't he try?"

"Not often," Julie said.

"I should steer clear of him then," Mrs Winters said, and Julie laughed. But later, when she was in her room tackling her homework she kept thinking about Matt and Craig, wondering what had caused the animosity between them. It was obvious that the dislike was not one-sided. Craig didn't like Matt any more than Matt liked him.

She knew they'd both gone to the same school and toyed with the idea that the feeling between them was merely because they were so different. Matt fond of sport and Craig not interested in it. Matt with his caustic remarks had probably made fun of Craig when he showed up badly at some game or other, or if Craig had refused to take part.

Then she thought of Charles, another boy who, in spite of being the college egg-head and a hater of all kinds of outdoor activity, was a great friend of Matt's.

There must have been something deeper than that. Before completing her homework Julie had decided that it must definitely be a girl. But which girl? Not Madeleine, because they hadn't known her before college days.

She wondered where the girl was now. She must have chosen Craig instead of Matt. Was she still *the* girl in Craig's life? Julie was still wondering about them when she went to bed and dreamt she was in a beauty parade with Craig and Matt as the judges. All the girls except one were girls from the college and the odd one was always in the shadows so that Julie couldn't see her properly. Julie dreamt that Madeleine was elected as Carnival Queen and Julie herself received only one vote – Matt's!

"How many votes did I get?" Cathy laughed, when Julie recounted the dream to her the next day.

They were on the way to the refectory for lunch and Julie could see Madeleine and Craig ahead of them. He had his hand on Madeleine's shoulders and they were talking animatedly. Julie couldn't help admiring them. They looked such an attractive pair and she wished Craig's hand had been on her shoulder instead of on Madeleine's.

After lunch, Craig came across to Julie and asked her to go to the Common Room with him to discuss the magazine. There were several other groups there making arrangements for the various activities and Craig led her to a corner and showed her some drawings.

"Some of the students in the art class have done these. They're designs for the cover of the magazine."

He handed them to Julie and thinking he wanted her to help choose the most suitable she picked one out. "I like this the best," she said.

Craig took it from her. "Maddy and I have already decided on the one we think most suitable," he said, "this is what I wanted to see you about, Julie." He handed her a sheet of paper covered with handwriting. "Will you type this for me, love? Correct spelling mistakes and that kind of thing, won't you?"

"I'll do it during afternoon break if Miss Compton will let me stay in the typing room."

Craig gave her a quick kiss on the cheek. "I'm sure she will – you're one of her favourites."

Dreamily Julie put her hand to the cheek Craig had kissed and saw Matt on the other side of the room looking at her. Their eyes met and he looked away quickly, but not before she'd seen the expression in them. What was it Cathy had said? That Matt always looked at her, Julie, as if he was saying goodbye to a friend!

She turned her attention back to Craig, who was saying, "We're casting the play tonight, are you coming?"

"Of course . . . if only to vote for you as the hero."

Craig looked pleased. "Why don't you volunteer for a part, Julie?"

"It's not my scene," she said and they both laughed at

the unintended pun.

The play had already been chosen and they were discussing it, their heads close together when Craig stopped speaking in the middle of a sentence. Looking up, Julie saw that he'd gone pale and was staring across the room at a girl who had just entered, a dark, pretty girl, rather shy-looking and intimidated by the crowd.

"Who is she, Craig?" Julie asked.

"How should I know." The papers he was holding dropped from his hands and he began to fumble about on the floor for them. Julie watched as Matt went up to the girl, took her hand and led her through the various chatting groups to the students from the design department. He introduced her then went back to his own group.

"Matt must know her," Julie said.

"Matt thinks he knows everything," Craig said acidly.

The bell prevented further conversation and the students went back to their respective classrooms. There were to be internal exams soon and, as Cathy said, their noses were being pressed to the grindstone even more firmly than usual. With that and the preparations for the summer celebrations there was little time left for anything else.

That evening those interested in the play were back in

the college theatre, admiring and criticising the students with acting ambitions who were being auditioned.

Several of the teachers were there and Julie was surprised to see the theatre at least half full. The play promised to be the highlight of the summer activities.

Miss Compton, who taught English and Drama as well as typewriting, and Mr Burgin, Public Speaking tutor, were the main judges and had the last say on the choice of actors but the students themselves were invited to show their approval by their applause.

Andrew, tall and thin, was chosen as the villain. He made everyone laugh by overacting in the old-fashioned melodramatic style. He'd stuck a moustache on his upper lip and wore a top hat he'd found in the props room. He was an easy choice – just right for the part.

Everyone expected Madeleine to be picked as the heroine and she was. She read her piece with just the right shade of feeling and Julie admired her assurance and ability.

"Wish I could be like that," she whispered to Cathy. "No wonder the boys fall for her."

"But none of them last," Cathy said wisely.

There were several volunteers for the hero's role, but Craig was the obvious choice. Not only was he good looking but he could act too. There were numerous 'ooh's' and 'ah's' from the girls as he played a short scene with Madeleine and he was easily the best of those auditioned.

He came to sit beside Julie as students were tested for the smaller parts.

"Congratulations," Julie whispered, "you were great."

"Thanks . . . I hope to do better on the night." He gave a sidelong glance, "And I will if you are on the front row rooting for me."

Julie felt pleased at the thought that he wanted her there. "I will be," she promised.

Suddenly Craig said, "Let's get out of here, Julie. It's boring, isn't it? Come on, my bike's outside, I'll take you for a spin."

"I've no helmet," Julie pointed out.

"No trouble, I'll borrow one. Bob Melling's brought his girlfriend and he's left theirs on a chair at the back of the hall."

"But suppose they want to leave before we get back?"

"They won't . . . Bob will be one of the last to be auditioned. We'll just go for a quick spin then I'll drop you home and return the helmet."

Craig pulled her up from her seat and although Julie had qualms about the whole thing the thought of being alone with Craig subdued them. She'd never expected him to ask her out – not with Madeleine there just waiting for Craig to offer to take her home. Quickly she whispered to Cathy, asking her to explain to Bob.

They soon left the town and sped down the country lanes. Clinging to Craig with her arms tightly round his waist and the wind whistling round her helmet was exciting and exhilarating. But as they got further away from the town Julie began to worry, and shouted to Craig to turn back. He made no response and she realised he couldn't hear her so she tugged on his waist and at last he drew into the kerb. Swivelling round he faced her.

"What's wrong, aren't you enjoying it?"

"Every minute, but we ought to go back, Craig. The audition will be nearly over and Bob . . ." She knew Bob as a big, red-haired lad with a fiery temper. He was one of Matt's fellow students in the engineering section.

"Forget Bob," Craig said, "all I want is to be alone with you, Julie."

"There'll be other times," she said, "please, Craig."

Reluctantly he restarted the bike and they sped back towards town. He drew up in front of Julie's house and she handed him the helmet.

"I'll go back to college and put the helmet where we

found it."

"Suppose Bob's waiting for it."

"Hard luck for Bob! Do him good to have to wait, he's too much of a bully boy for my liking."

Craig put his arms round her and kissed her lightly.

"I'll call for you one evening," he said.

The sound of a motorbike screeching to a standstill opposite, drowned Julie's reply. Bob Melling jumped off, raced across the road and grabbed Craig by the front of his sweater. His face was contorted with fury. "Who the devil do you think you are—going off with my girl's helmet?" He began to shake Craig, and Julie pulled at his arm as she tried to explain.

"It's not Craig's fault, Bob. He took it for me . . . he was just going to bring it back."

Bob shook her hand off his arm and stuck a clenched fist under Craig's nose. Julie stifled the scream which sprang to her lips.

"You think you're one hell-of-a-fella, don't you?" With each word he shook Craig. "Trying it on again aren't you, Craigie? But this is once too often." He drew back his huge fist as if he was going to thrust it into Craig's face. Julie hung on to his arm and at that moment heard the sound of feet racing down the road. The next moment Matt and Andrew flung themselves on to the two struggling boys and pulled them apart. With a sigh of relief Julie sat on the wall and watched as Matt calmed Bob down.

Andrew brought Bob's bike from across the road and Bob got on it. With a baleful glance at Craig he said, "One more dirty trick from you, Merton, and . . ."

"On your way, Bob," Matt said soothingly. Then as Bob kicked the engine into life, he added with a touch of the bitter sarcasm which Julie hated, "You can work out your anger on him in the play seeing as you've got the part of the tough guy. You can enjoy the fight scene with Craig!"

Furiously, Julie turned on Matt.

"Why on earth did you say that? You deliberately put the idea into Bob's mind, didn't you? You know what a hot-head he is. Matthew Dunning . . . I hate you!"

She raised her hand and slapped Matt hard across the face, then felt horror stricken as she saw the red weal appear on his cheek.

Matt caught her wrist and held it so tightly that she winced. "Thanks, Julie," he said, "your concern for him does you credit." He shot a contemptuous glance in Craig's direction, and he and Andrew walked away leaving Julie trembling. Whether it was from fear, anger or sympathy for Craig, she couldn't decide.

Chapter Five

MATT'S GIRL?

The following morning when Julie arrived at the college she found Bob Melling waiting to apologise for the previous evening's trouble.

"I'm sorry it had to involve you, Julie, but Viv's aunt was visiting them and I'd promised to have her back home before she left. I hope your mum and dad didn't hear the row we made outside your house."

"Luckily they were out and my sister was watching the telly. How did you know who'd taken the helmet?"

"Cathy – you asked her to tell me, didn't you? I'm glad you did."

Julie nodded. "Craig should have asked you," she said, "but he thought you wouldn't be leaving until later."

"*You* can think that if you like, Julie, but I know

49

better. He was having another go at me . . . and it had better be the last."

Fear struck Julie at the implied threat. "Please, Bob, don't do anything silly will you? Promise me . . ."

"I make no promises. Just tell *him* to keep his nose clean where I'm concerned, or else . . ." He walked away but Julie followed him. There was something she had to know.

"Bob," she caught hold of his arm, halting him as he strode down the corridor. "Why is Matt so mad with Craig?"

He didn't stop walking. "Better ask Matt that – it's none of my business." As he moved away she stared after him thoughtfully, wondering what it was that made Craig unpopular with the other lads. She put the question to Cathy later and Cathy, with her usual common-sense said, "It's obvious. He's so good-looking none of the others stand a chance – it's just male jealousy."

"I think there's more to it than that," Julie mused, "perhaps the girls themselves. They do flutter round him don't they?"

"Mm . . ." Cathy laughed, "present company not excepted!"

The desk next to Julie's was empty that morning.

Craig was preparing for a shorthand exam later that week.

Julie typed mechanically, her mind on the previous evening. If Miss Compton had asked her what her fingers had printed on the paper she wouldn't have been able to say.

She'd taken Craig into the house after the other boys had left and he'd had a quick, refreshing shower. "To wash the smell of that thug away," he'd said. Then, once more his usual charming self, he'd had supper with her and Emma, to the latter's delight.

"Aren't you the lucky one?" Emma had said after he'd gone. "Fancy him picking you out of all the girls in the college."

Craig was waiting for her in the refectory at the mid-morning break. He seemed to have forgotten about the previous night and Julie didn't remind him of it.

He'd already bought her a coffee and it wasn't until she took the seat he'd saved for her that she realised that Matt was at the next table and she was directly facing him.

She tried to catch his eye, wanting to smile her apology for the way she'd reacted the previous night but Matt appeared to be deliberately avoiding looking at her. She felt a twinge of sadness and wished she hadn't acted so hastily. Then she reminded herself that this was what she'd wanted. Hadn't she said to Cathy several times that she hoped he'd keep out of her way? If that slap on the cheek turned him off her – well, jolly good.

Craig snapped his fingers in front of her face, interrupting her thoughts. "Are you back with me?" he asked.

"Sorry, Craig, what were you saying?"

"I was asking if I could invite myself to your house again next Saturday. I'd like to meet your parents."

Julie's eyes lit up. The most fancied boy in the college actually asking her to take him home. "Of course. Mum will be chuffed, to say nothing of Emma," she assured him.

There was a movement on the next table. Andrew was giving up his chair to someone . . . it was the girl with dark hair whose appearance in the Common Room yesterday had turned Craig pale and made Matt go rushing to welcome her.

Matt smiled at the girl affectionately, then brought her a coffee. Suddenly Craig pushed his chair back and stood up. "Let's get out of here," he said, "it's stifling."

Julie encountered Matt only once more that day and the meeting was unavoidable. She was on her way to the language laboratory for the next lesson and was rounding the corner quietly when a hurrying figure sent her flying. Her head banged against the wall, and she dropped the papers she was carrying. Then a pair of strong arms steadied her.

"Fancy bumping into you," a familiar teasing voice said, "it must be fate."

Julie was surprised at the surge of relief which swept through her. Impulsively she said, "I'm sorry, Matt . . . about hitting you I mean." She put a gentle hand on the cheek she'd slapped and before she could take it away he put his own hand over hers, holding it there.

"I'm sorry too, Julie."

"It was such a fuss about nothing," Julie said regretfully. "Craig really did intend getting the helmet back before the end of the audition."

"It wouldn't have been something about nothing if Vivien had gone on the bike without the helmet – suppose they'd had an accident?" Matt pointed out. "No wonder Bob was furious."

"You don't think Bob will rake it up again, do you? I'm worried about the play . . . suppose he acts that fight for real."

"And gives lover-boy a bloody-nose you mean." Matt burst out laughing. "I wish I had his chance."

"You're always mocking. Why can't you be serious

for once," Julie said angrily. "I don't know why I bother."

Matt held his face on one side and pointed to his cheek. "Want to whack me again?" he said.

Flashing blue eyes stared into laughing brown ones for a moment then suddenly the smile disappeared from Matt's face. "What do you want me to do, Julie? Act as Craig's bodyguard so that he doesn't get his pretty face bruised?"

"Talk to Bob so that all the tension's gone before the play begins. It was you who put the idea into his mind in the first place."

Matt retrieved the last of Julie's papers from the floor and didn't speak until he'd watched her tuck them into her folder. "Look, Julie," he said, "I'll do anything for *you* but Craig doesn't need my help. He's big enough to stand on his own two feet."

As Julie walked away he called after her, "It's you I'm worried about."

"What an exasperating person he is," Julie thought. "He says a lot and yet tells me so little. What right has he to be worried about me?"

54

Chapter Six

LAND OF MAKE-BELIEVE

The various rooms in the college were all hives of industry in the evenings as well as the daytime now. Evening classes were over until the next term began but in the woodwork room students were making canvas frames for the scenery then passing them on to the art studio to be painted.

In the fashion and design department the chatter of sewing machines could be heard, as the costumes for the amateur actors and actresses were cut, fitted and sewn.

Already the electricians were fixing spotlights, footlights and numerous switches in the theatre hall. On most evenings Matt was there, supervising these arrangements.

Even the typewriting room had its part to play, with students typing and duplicating copies of each actor's part and programmes also had to be designed and typed.

During one of the rehearsals Miss Compton called Julie who was acting as prompter and Cathy took her place. "How would you like to understudy Madeleine's part?" Miss Compton asked.

Julie was staggered. "I couldn't do it, Miss Compton. Besides, it won't be necessary, will it – Madeleine's not likely to be off."

"You can never be sure. It's as well to have someone and I've already fixed a substitute for Craig if he happened to be off."

"But why me, Miss Compton, I've not even been auditioned for a part?"

"No, but with all the prompting you've done, you know most of the play off by heart already. Also Craig likes you, and liking the person you're acting with is a bonus." She smiled. "Can you imagine having to pretend you're in love with someone you don't like?"

"I don't suppose it would be very pleasant," Julie laughed, "but Craig likes Madeleine quite a lot."

"Of course he does – she's an attractive girl, but . . ." Miss Compton's voice dropped to a confidential whisper, "they do try to upstage each other, don't they?"

Julie had only seen Madeleine and Craig on stage

together once and couldn't bear to watch them again. Not because their acting was over the top but because it was too realistic. How could she watch Craig showing such tenderness to another girl even though it was only make-believe?

"You're the best choice for Madeleine's understudy," went on Miss Compton. "Think it over and let me know."

Cathy called round at Julie's home later that evening and the two girls took it in turns to dictate passages from their shorthand books then compare their speeds.

Later Mrs Winters came into the room with a tray of refreshments. "Have a break now, girls – you must be ready for a drink after all that reading aloud," she said.

Gratefully they put their books aside and settled down for a chat.

"Do you think we'll pass the eighty words a minute?" Cathy asked.

"Should do. Here's hoping anyway."

"Craig's coming round on Saturday," Julie said suddenly and Cathy looked surprised.

"Really! What about your resolution . . . no dates this year?"

"Well, Saturdays are an exception, aren't they!"

"So you're weakening?"

"I'm not. I'm just as determined as ever. More so now."

"Why more so?" Cathy wanted to know but Julie merely shrugged her shoulders. Even Cathy might not understand that to be the kind of girl Craig admired you'd have to be as ambitious as he was.

Although the play was to be one of the last of the charity events, the drama committee decided to have a dress-rehearsal on the following Saturday morning. Miss Compton pointed out that if they didn't they'd be crowded out by other events.

"It's the sponsored walk next Saturday," she said, "then two weekends are taken up with open days."

"What about one evening?" one boy asked, obviously thinking of the sport he'd been missing.

"Not practical. You're all involved in other things in the evening. Fortunately, most of the costumes are completed, but at the rehearsal the players will only wear them for the final scene."

They all crowded into the theatre that morning.

"I'll act as prompter," Miss Compton told Julie and Cathy, "then you two can watch the play."

Matt was busy with the spotlights but Julie saw the dark-haired girl sitting two rows in front of her. There was an empty seat beside her and on it lay Matt's jacket.

58

"Who is she?" Julie voiced her thoughts aloud.

"Don't know, except she's called Anne. She's in fashion and design and she's made some of Maddy's dresses."

Julie's heart fluttered when Craig made his first appearance. "Doesn't he look great?" she whispered to Cathy.

"You're not the only one who thinks so," Cathy laughed as the applause from the girls in the audience filled the auditorium. But Julie noticed that the girl in front of them was not clapping.

Madeleine was greeted with loud wolf whistles as soon as she walked on stage. "She does look gorgeous, doesn't she?" Cathy whispered. "Stunning," Julie replied.

Anxiously, Julie waited for the fight scene when Bob Melling as the rejected lover attacked Craig. As the fight scene began she clutched Cathy's arm until her friend winced. Matt, high up at the back of the hall working on the lights, plunged the stage into shadows simulating a dusky street scene. Craig, the hero, walked on, unaware that his enemy, Bob, was lurking in the shadows.

Suddenly the tension lightened as a girl in the audience yelled out, "Look out, Craig, he's waiting for you!"

Everyone dissolved into laughter except Craig who

turned furiously to face the audience. The scene was ruined. Matt turned the lights full on, and Bob, his rugged face creased with laughter, came out of his hiding place. Laughter echoed round the hall. Miss Compton, obviously trying to stifle her own laughter, emerged from the wings. The only person not amused was Craig, and Julie's heart ached for him. How awful to be tensed up as he must have been, then to have everything ruined by one stupid girl.

Miss Compton held up a hand for silence. "All right, you've had your fun – now let's get on with it. This is a play not a pantomime and I don't want any repetition." She looked sternly round the auditorium. "You don't make the actors' jobs any easier when you interrupt a scene like that – understood?"

The play resumed and the scene went off perfectly. Julie realised that the episode had released Bob's tension as it had her own. Bob aimed his punches in the air or where they wouldn't hurt and Craig feigned injury very realistically, falling gracefully on to the stage. Madeleine came running in looking prettier than ever and cried realistically over Craig. Julie wondered if he was enjoying this part as much as he seemed to be. If not, he was a very good actor indeed.

Chapter Seven

EVENING OF DEEP DISAPPOINTMENT

Craig arrived promptly at Julie's home at seven o'clock that same evening. Julie wore a new dress, one she'd chosen because she thought it was the kind Craig would like. She was excited, wondering where he'd be taking her, and wanting to sparkle that evening, just as Madeleine had done in the play.

Deep down she had a faint feeling of disquiet when she thought of the final tender scene between Craig and Madeleine. It had seemed as if both of them were playing it for real. Later she'd sought out Miss Compton and told her that she'd be Madeleine's understudy.

The teacher was pleased. "Good girl – you probably won't be needed but one never knows."

Secretly, Julie was hoping that she'd be asked to do at least one rehearsal with Craig for that was the only reason she'd offered. How wonderful it would be if she could play that final scene with him. She felt sure that given a chance like that, some kind of chemistry would spring up between them that would show Craig how right they were for each other.

When the doorbell rang, Julie was fixing her earrings, dangly ones similar to those Madeleine had worn in the play. She raced downstairs, and flung the door wide.

"Come in, Craig," she said, a smile on her pretty face as she leaned forward anticipating a kiss. Craig didn't seem to notice. "Hi, Julie," he said, stepping in and unwinding his scarf.

She introduced him to her parents and they chatted for a few moments. Julie wondered what plans he had for the evening and noticing his casual clothes began to feel sorry she'd gone to such trouble to dress up.

As her mother handed Craig a cup of tea he placed a folder on the table and her spirits dropped. Was this to be a 'working' evening? Tiny suspicions were forming in her mind. Did he come to her only when he needed help? Where did he spend his other spare evenings? With Madeleine?

Julie's father switched on the television for the news and Emma went to her bedroom to do her homework. Mrs Winters, obviously very taken with Craig, asked,

"What are you two going to do? I'm sure you don't want to stare at the box all evening."

Craig flashed his attractive smile at her, "I'm hoping Julie will help me with one or two things." He turned to Julie, and she couldn't resist the pleading look in his eyes, "She always does, you know." He turned to her mother again, "She's my right-hand man."

"So that's what I am," Julie thought.

They went into the sitting-room, Craig brought out his papers and they worked together for a time on a mock English exam he'd brought.

"English will be important to me in my job," he said.

"It will be in mine, too."

"Good, then this is helping you too, isn't it!"

When they'd completed the paper, Craig said, "Will you hear me say the last scene of the play, Julie? There's one part I'm not sure of. Did you notice?"

"I thought you were word-perfect."

"I faltered a bit but I'm glad you didn't notice."

Julie's spirits rose a little.

"You want me to act Madeleine's part?"

"No. Just read it aloud and see that I come in at the right places."

"Big deal," Julie murmured to herself.

"Tell you what, perhaps Emma could read some of

the parts."

Julie was surprised to see how eager Craig was to bring someone else into the evening which she'd looked forward to so much.

"Emma's doing homework."

"I know, but I'll bet she'd rather do this."

So, to her delight, Emma was brought down to read some of the other parts. They went over and over the same scene until Craig thought he'd got everything exactly right.

"Why don't you two act it instead of reading it and I'll be your audience?" Emma suggested.

Craig replied quickly, "Julie would have to read it from the book and it would sound stilted." Julie didn't bother to tell him that she knew the part as well as Madeleine did.

With a feeling of deep disappointment Julie went to the door with Craig. Sensing her mood he said, "We'll make up for tonight the next time we meet – I promise." But Julie was beginning to wonder if any of Craig's promises were kept. She went up to bed that night, took off the dress she'd put on so happily a few hours earlier and tossed it on to a chair. Craig hadn't even noticed it and she knew she'd never wear it again.

Chapter Eight

MADDY'S FIT OF TEMPER

The next college day was a prickly one for Julie. She was sitting alone in the Common Room, quietly reading through the play, when Madeleine came up to her, her eyes flashing angrily.

"Making yourself word-perfect so that you can take over my part, are you?"

Julie closed the book and looked at the other girl in surprise. "I've been asked to understudy you, if that's what you mean."

"Asked to! That's rich! You mean you begged for the part. You can't wait to get on the stage with Craig, can you?"

"Madeleine, be fair. Someone has to do it and Miss Compton asked me."

"Miss Compton nothing. You volunteered. Just as

you offered to help Craig with the magazine."

"I . . ." Julie began to deny the accusation but before she could say any more Madeleine interrupted, "And even that wasn't enough, was it? You offered to help him with his homework too."

"Who told you all this?"

"Never you mind." Madeleine's pretty face was flushed with anger as she glared at Julie accusingly.

"You're hoping right now that I'll be ill when the play's put on, aren't you? Or better still that I'll have an accident on the sponsored walk."

Julie stared at her in surprise. "You're not going on the walk, are you?"

"If Craig is then I am." Madeleine stalked away but turned round when she reached the door. "Somehow," she said, "I can't imagine you playing my part – you just wouldn't look right."

Julie was stunned. Questions were rushing through her mind. How could Madeleine have got to know about the homework sessions with Craig except from Craig himself? She brushed the thought away. If he had mentioned it, he would have done so in the ordinary course of conversation – he could have had no idea that Madeleine would react in the way she had.

She wondered if Madeleine had taken his acting for real. Did she think that the words he said on stage in his character part were really meant for her – Madeleine?

Suddenly, Julie became aware of a slight movement in the far corner of the large room. Someone was sitting there silently, hidden by the high back of the chair which faced the room.

Julie, embarrassed that someone must have heard Madeleine's bitter words, walked across, her footsteps deadened by the carpet. To her surprise she found herself looking down at Anne, the girl to whom Matt had behaved so protectively. The girl smiled apologetically. "I'm sorry," she said, "I couldn't help hearing. I was here when you came in but you didn't notice me."

Julie felt relieved that it wasn't Matt or Craig. She felt she could trust this girl.

"You're Julie, aren't you? Matt's told me about you," Anne said. On her knee was a beautiful dress of silver brocade. She held it up for Julie's inspection. "I'm just adding the finishing touches," she said. "It's for Madeleine's last scene and I'd arranged to meet her here for a fitting."

"It's lovely." Julie fingered the sparkling material. "Aren't you clever?"

"Well, it's my job. I work part-time for a fashion house and come here the rest of the week."

"I'd better leave you if Madeleine's coming back for a fitting," Julie began to walk away but Anne called her back.

"Can I fit it on you instead, Julie? I don't think Madeleine will come back now – she's probably forgotten all about it. She *was* in a temper, wasn't she?"

"She'll be in an even worse one if she gets to know I've

had the dress on."

"She won't get to know, I promise. She'll be rehearsing now and I can get on with it in class if I know it's O.K." She was already slipping the dress over Julie's head. "It's only the length which needs adjusting and you're both the same height, aren't you?"

The dress was beautiful and Julie twirled round in it, trying to see her reflection in the windows. Then she stood still while Anne on hands and knees pinned up the hem to the required length.

"What a lot of trouble to go to just for three or four performances," Julie said.

"It'll be put in the props room so it will probably be used for other plays." Anne took the last pin out of her mouth, stuck it in the dress and smiled up at her. "I've enjoyed making it – it's good practice for me."

A voice broke into their conversation, "What luck finding my two favourite girls together." It was Matt and he stood for a moment staring at Julie who couldn't decide whether he was admiring her or the dress.

"Were you looking for Julie or me?" Anne asked. Matt replied, "You."

Julie felt a sense of disappointment and realised to her surprise that she would have been pleased if Matt had said she was the one he wanted. Their paths hadn't crossed much recently, probably she thought because he was spending as much time as he could with Anne.

"What did you want?" Anne asked.

"Only to say I won't be able to take you home tonight – I'm staying on here."

"O.K." Anne replied, folding the dress carefully. "Now I must fly, I'm due back in class and it's a ten minute walk to the fashion studios."

"Bye love," Matt said. "See you."

Julie went to pick up her book, "I must be off too."

"I'm thinking of volunteering to understudy Craig," Matt said quietly.

"You!" Julie turned in surprise. Matt was the last person she could imagine wanting to act. "But you're in charge of the lights."

"They're all fixed now and there are plenty of others who can see to that side of it."

"But why? I would have thought Bob's role would have suited you better seeing how you feel about Craig."

Matt laughed. "So that I could have had a bash at him you mean?" He paused for a moment. "No, Julie, I'm only doing it because I heard you're doing the same for Madeleine – can't you just picture us two as the hero and heroine?"

"Come off it, Matt. We'd be scratching each others'

eyes out if we were on stage together."

"I know I'm like a red rag to a bull where you're concerned, Julie – but you looked great in that dress and suddenly I wanted to be in on the act."

"Madeleine will look better in it."

"Not to me."

"You're always leg-pulling, Matt." She walked out of the room, not knowing whether to believe Matt or not. "I never know when to take him seriously," she thought. Besides, there was obviously a thing going between him and Anne. Julie had seen them waiting for each other on most evenings and then walking off together. She couldn't imagine him two-timing anyone but if Anne was his girl friend he shouldn't be showing interest in anyone else. She'd keep out of Matt's way in future, she decided, beginning to feel fed up with the tangles which seemed to be surrounding her.

She went into her classroom and took her place next to Cathy.

"Where've you been?" the latter wanted to know.

"I've just been ticked off by Madeleine and pestered by Matt. The next thing to happen will be the last straw."

"I doubt it. Craig's been looking for you."

Julie's spirits rose. "Did he say why?"

"No, only that he'll be in that little room in the tower

block this afternoon. You know, where the duplicating machines are."

Julie made her way to the lift during the afternoon break, pressed the button and waited for it to come down. When the lift door opened she was surprised to see Anne walk out.

"Hi," she said, noticing that the other girl looked upset.

"Hello, Julie," Anne said, before the lift closed again and Julie was whisked up to the top of the tower block.

"Just the girl I wanted to see," Craig said, "I'm up to the eyes with this lot."

"So that's why you wanted to see *me*?"

She stressed the last word and Craig looked at her in surprise, then took hold of her hands. "Look, Julie, you know I'm always glad to see you but there's not been much time lately." He pinched her cheek playfully. "The real reason is because I wanted an excuse to get you up here so that we could be alone together for a bit."

A feeling of happiness surged inside her. Being with Craig always made her feel like this but knowing that he wanted to be with her made it even better.

"Mr Burgin will be back in a few minutes, he's designing the programme, but there's something I wanted to ask you."

"What?"

"I'm practically sure I've passed the shorthand exam and I want to take you out to celebrate and thank you for helping."

"You don't have to thank me for that."

"Julie – I want to."

Julie's resolve weakened. "All right, Craig. When and where?" She thought of their previous evening together and the dress she'd bought for the occasion. Ruefully she wondered if she wore jeans and a top would the reverse happen and Craig take her somewhere romantic.

"I'll tell you later." Craig went to a cupboard and produced a tube of duplicating ink. "You've only got ten minutes now, Julie. Could you put this ink in that wretched duplicating machine. It's run dry on me and you know how to refill it."

She stared at him aghast, her illusions cracking slowly and painfully.

"Craig! That's the dirtiest job in college. Everyone hates doing it and I've got an English lesson in ten minutes."

"It'll only take you five minutes . . . please, Julie, love." He held his hands out. "I'd do it myself but I'm checking these papers. They've been sent in for the magazine and it takes ages to get the ink off your hands." His eyes pleaded with her and she knew she couldn't refuse. "Please, Julie, love, you'll do a little thing like that for me, won't you?"

Mr Burgin came in at that moment and seeing Julie said, "Good, we can do with a little help."

"Julie's only got ten minutes but she's going to put the ink in the duplicator."

"Good girl. Filthy job. No-one ever wants to do it."

After that there was nothing she could do except get on with the job, but later as she scrubbed her hands trying to get off the stains she knew she was trying to scrub Craig from under her skin at the same time.

"I'm a fool," she muttered to herself. "I should have kept to my resolution. No boys, no dates, no involvements." She finished drying her hands then looked at her watch and realised she was late for English. Angrily, she crumpled up a paper towel and flung it into the bin. "Goodbye, Craig Merton," she murmured to herself.

Chapter Nine

LOCKET OF LOVE

Saying goodbye to Craig, however, was another resolve Julie was going to find hard to keep. He was waiting for her at the door of the college when she left.

"I'm sorry, Julie," he said immediately, "I shouldn't have asked you to do that filthy job." When he smiled at her like that her heart quickened and she felt hope surging inside her again. They walked hand in hand until they reached the well-lit road. Stopping beneath a street lamp, Craig took a small box from his pocket and handed it to Julie.

"It's not my birthday," she said, surprised.

"This is an un-birthday present," Craig said. "You don't have to have an excuse to show someone how much you like them, do you?"

She pressed the button on the box and the lid flew

back. Inside was a slender, silver bracelet with a tiny heart attached to it.

"Oh, Craig," Julie said, "it's lovely."

"I bought it because I thought it was just right for you," Craig said tenderly.

He unfastened the clasp and put it on Julie's wrist. "Like it?"

"I love it. Thank you, Craig. I'll wear it always."

He squeezed her hand. "Not always, Julie. Keep it for special occasions – when we're together."

"All right," Julie agreed. "It would probably catch on my typewriter anyway and I'd hate to damage it."

Before they parted. Craig took a sheaf of papers from his case. "You're still going to help me with this lot, aren't you, Julie? They're easy to read but I wouldn't have time to type them myself."

The word "bribery" crept into Julie's mind but she blotted it out quickly – it was unworthy of Craig.

"I'll do them at home on Dad's portable," she promised.

"Good. Then I'll call for them and this time we'll go out somewhere."

They parted and Julie went home in a glow of happiness. She'd been hard on Craig, she told herself. He'd taken a lot of work on and needed help with it and she should be feeling delighted that he'd chosen her to assist him instead of thinking that he was using her. She kept touching the box in her pocket to make sure that the last conversation with Craig had really happened. They'd said very little to each other really but Craig had implied that they'd be spending more time together in the future.

As she got ready for Craig's visit, thoughts of their last disastrous evening kept intruding. She didn't dress up as she had before but put on a neat skirt and pretty top. She recalled the outing on his bike and what it had led to, and shuddered. He wouldn't bring that again anyway – at least she hoped not.

When Craig arrived she gave him the work she'd typed and they chatted for a while with her parents. Then he announced, "I've got two tickets for the Civic Hall, Julie, there's a group playing there."

"Lovely," Julie said.

She'd been hoping they could go somewhere where they could talk and get to know each other. There seemed to be so little time in a college day for two people to be alone. In spite of that, she enjoyed the concert and as they walked to the bus afterwards, Julie said happily, "I'll see you tomorrow, Craig."

"The dreaded day," he moaned.

"You mean the sponsored walk? It shouldn't be too bad."

"Knowing you'll be there makes it better."

Julie looked up at him. "Does it really, Craig?"

"Course it does. But don't let Matt monopolise you, will you?"

Julie looked surprised. "Matt? Some hopes, he's got a girl, hasn't he?"

"Has he?" It was Craig's turn to look surprised.

There was a shock waiting for Julie when she arrived home. Sitting in the living-room, chatting to her parents, was Matt. She stared at him open-mouthed and Matt laughed at her expression.

"I expect I'm the last person you expected to see here," he said. "I tried to see you in college but you were a missing link."

"I went to the tower block in the afternoon break," Julie said. "Craig needed help with the duplicating."

"So you were the one to get your hands dirty this time." The words were simple but Julie knew there was some implication there. This made her want to protect Craig from such gossip.

Matt handed her a leaflet containing the route for the sponsored walk. It showed the various checkpoints where each walker's card would be marked.

Julie took Matt into the sitting-room so that her parents could watch the TV programme without interruption.

"I gave these leaflets out this afternoon," Matt told her, "and we had a short meeting after class but you and Craig had already left."

They discussed the walk for some time. "Prompt at the college gates at one o'clock," Matt said. "There's a pause for refreshments at the half-way stage," he pointed to a cross on the chart, "but there's no set time because we'll all walk at different rates."

Julie glanced at the leaflet. "It ends at the Moorland Hotel," she said. "Gosh, it's a climb up there."

"I'll help you," Matt promised.

"I think I'll be able to manage on my own two feet," Julie laughed.

"Even allowing for the slowest walkers, we should be at the hotel for five o'clock. Arrangements have been made for us to have a wash and to change into something more appropriate for dinner."

"I can't carry a change of clothes with me," Julie pointed out.

"That's another reason why I'm here. Andrew's arranged for a van to take all our things up, so if you'll give me yours I'll take them for you."

Thinking Matt thought of everything, Julie went upstairs and packed a small case with the things she'd need plus a make-up bag and earrings. She was looking forward to the walk yet couldn't get rid of a feeling of disquiet.

"Does Craig know of the arrangements?" she asked when she came down.

"Andrew's gone to put him in the picture and to collect his clothes." Suddenly Julie felt embarrassed at the way Matt was looking at her.

"Is there something wrong?" she asked.

"No. You look great!"

"Matt! I never know when to take you seriously."

"I feel I have to wear a shield when I'm with you, Julie."

"Like protective clothing? You once said I was too prickly."

Matt changed the subject. "Your mum told me you'd gone with Craig to see the group at the Civic Hall. Did you enjoy it?"

"So, so." There was another embarrassing silence then Julie asked, "Do we all start off in a bunch tomorrow or leave at set times in small groups?"

"It'll be more or less go as you please. We'll even out when we get going."

Julie walked with him to the door. "Thanks for taking all this trouble, Matt," she said as she handed him her case. He didn't reply and she noticed he was staring fixedly at the hand holding the case. He was looking at the bracelet on her wrist and the expression on his face was one of surprise and shock. Gripping her wrist, he twisted it round until he could see the silver heart dangling from the chain. Then he looked at her with eyes she couldn't fathom, almost as if he was pitying her. "I'm sorry it had to be you, Julie," Matt said. "Is Craig's photo still inside?"

He was gone before she could reply and Julie flew upstairs to take the bracelet off. Matt thought he'd seen it before but there must be hundreds of similar trinkets around. She examined the tiny heart more closely and saw that it was hinged. With a finger nail she prised it open and looked at the tiny picture of a smiling Craig. She wondered who had cut it from the original snap. Craig himself or . . . It showed only his head and one shoulder but on that shoulder she could just see a few brown curls. There must have been a girl on the original, standing beside Craig with her head on his shoulder.

"Well, what of it?" Julie asked herself. "Craig's bound to have had lots of girl friends. Then she remembered he'd said he'd bought the bracelet specially for her. Yet Matt obviously thought he'd seen it somewhere before!

There was an argument going on inside Julie's head. She was asking herself why she should believe Matt instead of Craig. She was trying hard to cling on to her beliefs but it was becoming more and more difficult.

Incidents which she'd almost forgotten were coming into her mind. How every time Craig had arranged to see her he'd needed her help in some way. Had that happened to Vivien, Bob's girl friend, too? Did Craig always use his charm to get things done for him?

Julie tossed and turned in bed that night, unable to sleep because of the confused thoughts chasing themselves through her mind. Suddenly she switched on her bedside lamp and reached for the bracelet again. She'd remembered how Anne had looked when she came out of the lift. Upset and tearful.

Julie opened the locket again. Yes, the brown hair on Craig's shoulder could be Anne's and a horrible thought came into her mind. Had Anne gone to the tower block to return the bracelet to Craig? And could Craig have turned such a situation to his own advantage on the spur of the moment? And, worse still, pretended he'd bought it specially for her – Julie. She flung the trinket from her and heard it clatter on her dressing-table.

Chapter Ten

PAINFUL TRUTH

Julie was up early in spite of her restless night. She knew now what she had to do – confront Craig with her suspicions. It wasn't fair to judge him without giving him the chance to defend himself.

Andrew, Cathy, Matt and Anne were already at the college gates when she arrived but she sat on the grass where she couldn't be seen, not feeling in the mood for talking. Cathy and Andrew were laughing at something the latter had said, making Julie realise how rarely she and Craig had shared a joke. Anne seemed to be having difficulty with her walking shoes and Julie saw Matt take them from her and untangle the laces.

They, too, were laughing, Matt on his knees looking up at Anne as he pushed the shoes on her feet and retied the laces. Julie could sense something special between them, a closeness which she envied as realisation dawned. She could have had Matt's friendship but she'd refused to let it develop. "Boys," she thought, "they're all the same. Even Matt pretended to like me when all the time he's tied up with Anne."

She had the bracelet clutched in her hand, willing Craig to come soon. She hoped he'd be alone so that they could sort out together the things which were worrying her.

Julie didn't know then that the day was to be one of shocks, misunderstanding and surprises.

Next to arrive were Bob and Vivien and they sat on the grass beside her.

"I'm waiting for Craig," she told them.

"And I'll bet that's the story of your life at the moment," Bob said. Vivien gave him a dig. "Shut up, Bob."

"Why does everyone clamp up when I mention Craig," Julie wanted to know.

"Why spoil a lovely day by talking about unpleasant subjects," was Bob's reply.

"Take no notice of him, Julie," Vivien said, "he's got a thing about Craig." On a sudden impulse Julie held out the bracelet, "Have you ever seen this before, Vivien?"

The other girl looked at the bangle then at Julie. "So it's your turn for the peace-offering now," was all she said.

They went to join the others giving Julie more food for thought. Vivien had red hair and she was certainly not the girl who had been on the original photograph with Craig. It must be Anne. That would explain Matt's feeling towards Craig. But she knew instinctively that Vivien, too, had once owned that bracelet.

She could see Craig approaching now with Madeleine. He had an arm round her shoulder and Julie couldn't help thinking how right they looked together. Julie stood up, Craig saw her and said something to Madeleine who walked on while he came up to Julie.

"Good news," he said, "I got my exam results this morning and I've passed – with a distinction."

Julie merely held out the bracelet saying, "I want to return this to you."

Craig looked surprised then Julie saw a suspicious gleam come into his eyes.

"Why? You said you liked it. I told you . . ."

"I know what you told me. That you'd bought it specially for me. Did you tell Vivien that, too, and Anne? And how many more girls have you said that to?"

Mentioning Anne was a shot in the dark but she knew

it was true when she saw the angry flush stain Craig's cheeks.

"So Matt's been blabbing, has he? He and his precious Anne."

"Anne gave the bracelet back to you just a couple of hours before you gave it to me, didn't she? Will Madeleine be the next one to wear it?"

"No, it's not good enough for her," Craig said as he snatched the box angrily.

"Will *she* be good enough to take over all the work I was going to do for you?"

Craig began to look alarmed. "You're not going to let me down, Julie. You can't at the last minute, there's stacks of typing to do. Please . . ."

"Madeleine can type, too," Julie pointed out, "but will she be willing to help with the duplicating machine, all that ink on her hands?"

Craig became conciliatory. "Look, I'm sorry, Julie. I'll come round to your house tomorrow and we'll clear things up, shall we?"

The old charm was there and Julie was as surprised as Craig to find it wasn't working. "Don't come round, Craig," she said, "I'll finish the typing and I'll give it to you on Monday."

Chapter Eleven

A NEW FUTURE

Julie walked with the group which contained Anne and Matt. Cathy was with Andrew who, as the organiser, felt he had to lead the way at the beginning at least. The day was bright with a cool sun, ideal conditions for a long walk. Julie, holding her face to the slight breeze felt as if she'd walked through a cloud and emerged into sunshine. She could see things clearer now as far as Craig was concerned, but there were still some anxieties lurking at the back of her mind. Things she'd said which she wished she could have unsaid. But not to Craig.

The walkers thinned out gradually according to their speed. The going grew tougher after a few miles and at each checkpoint one or two dropped out.

At one point Andrew called for Matt's help. A girl had fallen and cut her leg. Matt had some knowledge of first aid and Andrew wanted to stay in front as he was familiar with the route.

"Anne's squeamish about blood," Matt said. "How about you, Julie, will you help me?"

"Sure," Julie replied. Yet even as she spoke a thought flickered through her mind, "Is Matt another, wanting me with him only when I'm useful?"

The girl's leg was bleeding but the cut was not serious. Matt produced bandages from the kit he carried on his back and Julie helped him while he placed a pad on the wound and deftly wound a bandage round it.

"You'll live, Mary," he smiled as he helped the girl up. At that moment Julie heard the click of a camera and turned to see Craig standing just behind them. "That'll look fine in the colour pages," he said, "with all that blood around."

"You never miss a chance, do you?" Matt shouted angrily.

"Of course not," Craig replied coolly. "You don't think I came on this outing just to walk, do you? I'm on an assignment for my newspaper."

"So you're a newspaper tycoon now, are you?" Matt's voice was sarcastic.

"Not yet, but here's hoping."

Craig strolled off. Someone called Matt so Julie

walked on with Mary. There were cars at each check point and Mary said she'd get a lift to the hotel at the next one.

They'd reached the wooded part of the walk now. Twigs cracked as they walked and the sun made patterns through the foliage above them. Cathy was waiting for her in a clearing and said, "I can't keep up with Andrew now. I'm beginning to flake out." She stared at her friend, "I thought you'd have been with Craig."

"Craig's with Madeleine." Seeing her friend's look of sympathy she added, "It's all over between us."

"I'm glad, Julie. Everyone except you knew he was using you as a general dog's body. Craig just turns on the charm whenever he wants some help with anything. I'm lucky – he never tried it with me."

At the halfway cafe, Matt was waiting with cups of tea. He took Julie to a table outside and they sat down. Cathy spotted Andrew with a group studying the map and she went to join him.

"Are you all right, love?" Matt asked, his usually laughing face full of concern.

"Sure I am," Julie said, then with Matt looking so sympathetic and feeling she had to unburden her feelings on someone, she blurted out, "I'm just a bad judge of character, Matt. You never told tales about Craig but you tried to warn me and I just wouldn't listen to you."

"I'm not a tale-teller," Matt said, putting his hand over hers, "but I couldn't bear the thought of you being hurt like Anne was."

"You'd seen the bracelet before, hadn't you, Matt?"

Matt gave her hand a little squeeze, "Yes. And you've guessed, haven't you? Anne was in your shoes once. Number one with Craig just like you've been."

"What happened?" Julie whispered.

"They went to the same evening classes. Anne was brilliant and he soon cottoned on as he always does. He kept getting her to help him, especially when the exams were looming." Matt paused for a moment then continued, "Just like you did, Anne fell for all that soft soap. Then twice he made dates with her, promising to take her out and twice he didn't turn up."

Someone called to them to hurry up and join the walk but Matt made no attempt to move. "The second time he left Anne waiting for him was in town. She stood in the street for an hour and it was the night of a big football match. She got caught up with a lot of hooligans and was upset and frightened. I couldn't forgive him for that. All he had to do was phone her before she left home but he didn't have the guts to do that. There's only one thought in Craig's mind, how to climb over everyone else because he must get to the top first."

"Yet, in spite of all that, you didn't split on him – you're an unusual boy, Matt."

Matt grinned, "You're to blame for that, Julie. I couldn't imagine even Craig not wanting you so I didn't want to spoil things for you. Then when I saw him giving you all his dirty jobs to do while he was out with Madeleine I knew he was up to his old tricks again."

Julie changed the subject, "You're keen on Anne, aren't you, Matt?"

"Anne and I are twin spirits."

Julie smiled at him, "I hope things work out for you both," she said. "Anne's lucky."

"Are you ready for a few eye-openers?" Matt asked.

"Be serious for once, Matt."

"I'm dead serious," he replied, yet he seemed to be having difficulty holding his laughter in. "You're imagination's been working overtime, Julie. About Anne, I mean."

"Anne and Craig?"

Matt shook his head. "No Anne and me."

"But you said . . . Anne said . . ."

Matt could restrain his laughter no longer, "Anne is my cousin. We've known each other since the year dot."

"You said you were twin spirits," Julie stammered.

"So we are. We were born on the same day and my father and Anne's mother are brother and sister, and we live next door to each other. We're nearly twins in fact."

"Matt, you're pulling my leg."

"Ask Anne," Matt said. "I believe we shared the same pram – you can't get much closer than that, can you?"

Suddenly they were both laughing, sharing a truly happy moment.

The final week of term arrived before anyone was ready for it. On the last three days of that week the play was to be presented and as so many students were involved in one way or another, little work was done.

They went into the theatre hall and Matt took his place behind the spotlights while Julie went to the prompter's chair. It was a good thing that those taking part in the play were word-perfect for although Julie's eyes were on the printed page she didn't see the words because Matt's face kept intruding.

When the rounds of applause came at the end of the play after the final night's performance, Julie closed her book rather sadly, knowing that she would soon be saying goodbye to Matt. A new intake would be coming into the college at the beginning of next term but somehow she didn't think any one of them would replace Matt, either in the various committees he'd joined or in her affections.

She herself still had several months to stay on and she thought of the promise she'd made to herself at the beginning of the year. No boys, no dates, just hard work. She smiled to herself. Ahead of her were the summer holidays and somehow she knew Matt would be playing a large part in those. There was a time and a place for everything. Hard work could go hand in hand with pleasure, these past few months had proved that at any rate.

She struggled through the crush of people towards the entrance, certain that Matt would be waiting for her there. He was! The play was over, the make-believe and uncertainties were a thing of the past. This was for real.

Julie slipped her hand into Matt's confidently as they walked together to her home.

THE END